PEANUTS

SNOOPY™

ILLUSTRATED BY ART MAWHINNEY AND VICKI SCOTT

phoenix international publications, inc.

AS THE WORLD-FAMOUS AUTHOR, SNOOPY IS WRITING A NEW NOVEL. FIND THESE ELEMENTS OF HIS MYSTERY STORY.

DETECTIVE BADGE

THIS FLASHLIGHT

HANDCUFFS

MONOGRAMMED GLOVE

BINOCULARS

THIS BANDIT EYE MASK

THIS MAGNIFYING GLASS

THIS PAW PRINT

THE WORLD WAR I FLYING ACE MAKES HIS WAY AROUND THE GLOBE. CAN YOU FIND THESE CLOUDS THAT LOOK LIKE FAMOUS LANDMARKS HE HAS SEEN?

PARTHENON

LEANING TOWER OF PISA

COLOSSEUM

ARC DE TRIOMPHE

AZTEC PYRAMID

SPHINX

LINUS GAVE HIS BLANKET TO SNOOPY...BUT THEN HE WANTED IT BACK! LOOK FOR THESE FRIENDS THAT WILL TRY TO HELP LINUS FIND SNOOPY AND HIS BLANKET.

PIG-PEN

PATTY

CHARLIE BROWN

PEPPERMINT PATTY

MARCIE

ROY

IT'S SNOOPY'S BIRTHDAY! ALL OF HIS FRIENDS HAVE GOTTEN TOGETHER TO THROW A PARTY FOR THE WORLD-FAMOUS BEAGLE! GRAB SOME CAKE AND LOOK FOR THESE GIFTS.

BONE

BOW TIE

WATER DISH

THIS BLANKET

NEW COLLAR

NEW AIRPLANE GOGGLES

SNOOPY HITS SO MANY HOME RUNS, THE GANG ALWAYS NEEDS TO KEEP A FEW BASEBALLS HANDY. RUN BACK TO THE BASEBALL DIAMOND AND LOOK FOR ALL TEN OF THE TEAM'S BASEBALLS.

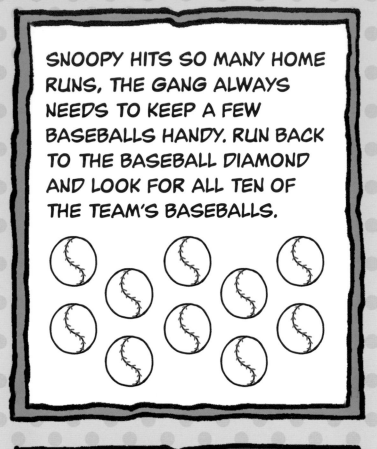

GO BACK TO SNOOPY AND HIS TYPEWRITER AND FIND THESE COMEDY PROPS THAT DON'T BELONG IN HIS MYSTERY NOVEL.

RUBBER CHICKEN

BULB HORN

CLOWN SHOE

CHATTERING TEETH

FAKE NOSE & EYEGLASSES

"CAN OF NUTS"

HIKE BACK TO THE CAMPSITE AND FIND ALL 44 BEAGLE SCOUTS.

SOAR BACK TO THE FLYING ACE AND LOOK FOR THE LETTERS THAT SPELL RED BARON!

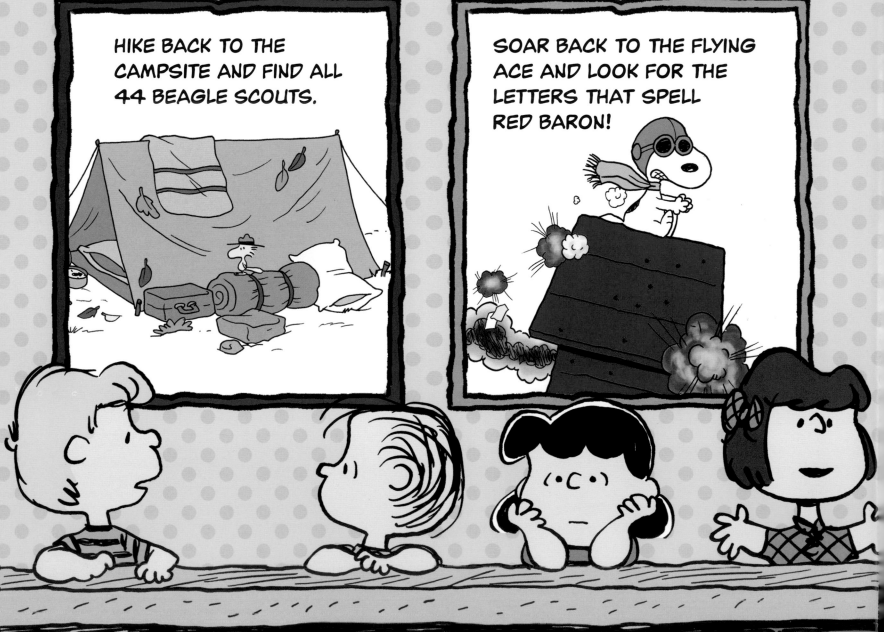

LINUS STILL CAN'T FIND SNOOPY OR HIS BLANKET ANYWHERE! GO BACK TO THE NEIGHBORHOOD MAZE AND HELP HIM FIND A PATHWAY THAT LEADS TO EVERYONE'S FAVORITE BEAGLE.

JOIN UP WITH JOE COOL IN THE SCHOOLYARD AND FIND THESE SUNGLASSES THAT HE IS TOO COOL TO WEAR.

HEAD BACK TO SNOOPY'S SUPPERTIME AND LOOK FOR THESE CANNED GOODIES.

RETURN TO SNOOPY'S BIRTHDAY AND LOOK FOR THESE PARTY MUST-HAVES.

PUNCH BOWL

THIS PARTY HAT

DOGHOUSE CENTERPIECE

THIS NOISE MAKER

PIÑATA

THIS SLICE OF CAKE